When Grandpa Died

Words by Margaret Stevens

Pictures by Kenneth Uland

 CHILDRENS PRESS, CHICAGO

1 2 3 4 5 6 7 8 9 10 11 12 R 85 84 83 82 81 80 79

Library of Congress Cataloging in Publication Data

Stevens, Margaret.
  When grandpa died.

  SUMMARY: A little girl tries to come to terms with
the death of her grandfather.
  [1. Death—Fiction. 2. Grandfathers—Fiction]
I. Ualand, Kenneth. II. Title.
PZ7.S84459Wn   [Fic]   78-12360
ISBN 0-516-02025-0

When Grandpa Died

When Grandpa lived with us, we did lots of things together.

Sometimes he would read to me. Or tell me funny stories about when he was a boy. Other times he and I would go for long walks.

But most of the time we worked in the garden together. Grandpa said I was the best helper he'd ever had.

Once we found a dead bird in the garden. It felt cold and hard when I touched it.

I asked Grandpa why the bird had died. Grandpa said he didn't know for sure. Maybe it was sick. Or maybe it was hurt. Or maybe it was very old and not strong enough to live any longer. Grandpa said there are many reasons why things die.

Then Grandpa told me to get a box. We put the bird inside. I put some soft cotton around the bird. Then Grandpa and I buried the box in the yard. We planted a flower to show where we had buried the bird.

Grandpa said that everything that is alive has to die sometime. He said that death is natural. Natural means that things turn out the way they are supposed to.

Then Grandpa told me that all living things keep growing and changing. Even after they die, they keep changing. Grandpa said that when the bird's body changed, it would help the flowers to grow.

Grandpa knew about lots of things.

Then one day Grandpa had to stay in bed. Mom said he was very sick. My little sister and I had to be very quiet so Grandpa could rest.

Sometimes I would sit in the chair by Grandpa's bed and watch him sleep.

Then one morning Grandpa got very, very sick. He had to go to the hospital.

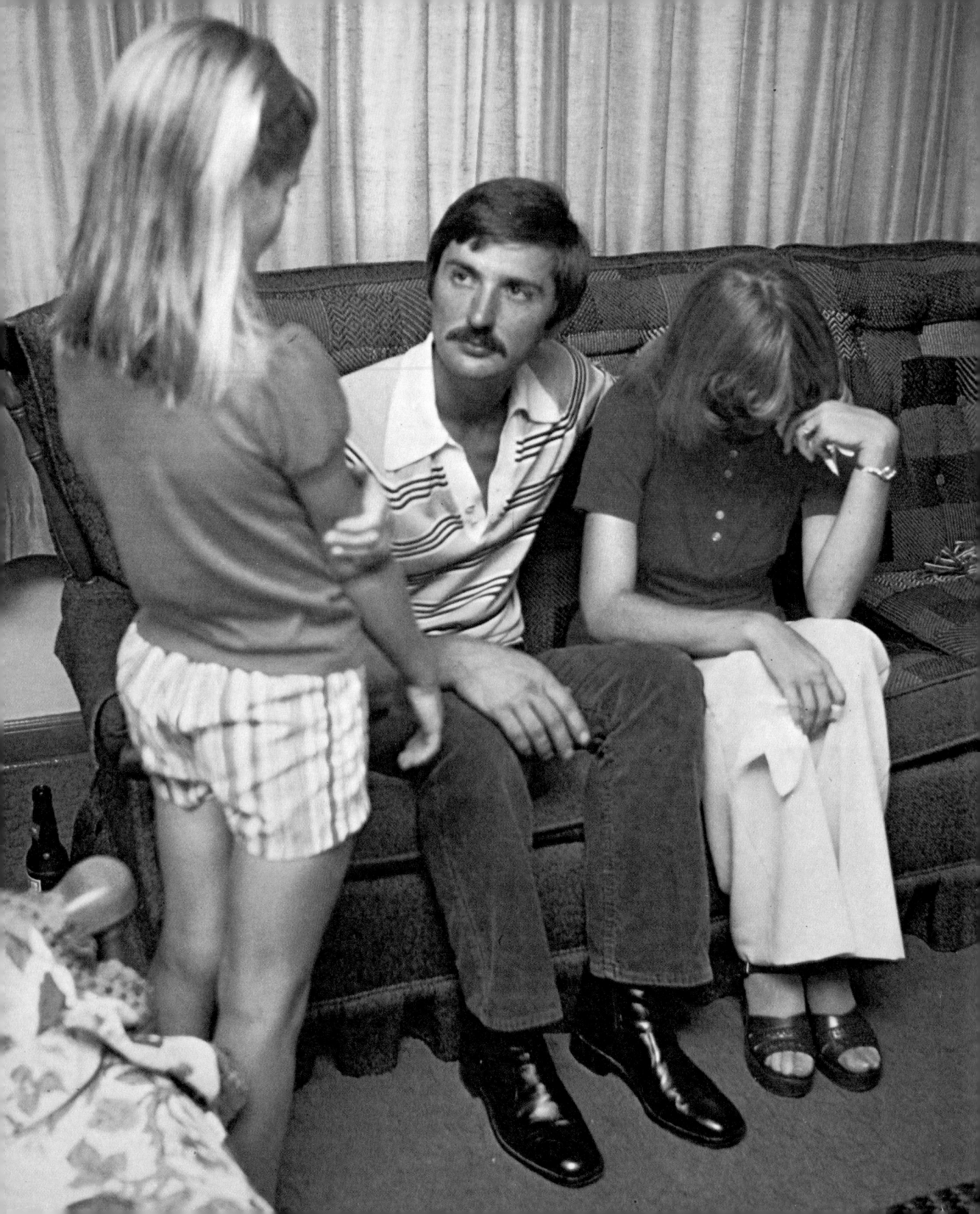

Mom and Dad went to see him in the hospital every day.

One day Mom was crying when they came home. Dad looked like he was going to cry too. I felt scared. I knew something bad had happened.

Then Dad told me that Grandpa was dead. I didn't cry. I felt mad. I was angry with Grandpa for dying. I didn't want him to die. I wanted him to come home and play with me.

I went into Grandpa's room and put on his sweater. I sat in the chair by his bed. Then I cried and cried.

Dad came into the room. He held me in his arms. He told me that it was okay to cry.

I told Dad I was sad because I never said good-bye to Grandpa.

Dad said that there would be a funeral for Grandpa. He said a funeral is where people can say good-bye to someone they love.

Dad took me to see the coffin that Grandpa would be buried in.

The next day we went to Grandpa's funeral.

I used to think that Grandpa would come back to live with us. Now I know he won't.

My sister is too little to understand about Grandpa. Someday when she's older, I'm going to tell her all about him.